YO GABBA GABBA!

LET'S USE OUR IMAGINATIONS!

BY IRENE KILPATRICK

ILLUSTRATED BY MIKE GILES

SIMON SPOTLIGHT

New York   London   Toronto   Sydney

Based on the TV series *Yo Gabba Gabba!*™ as seen on Nick Jr.®

SIMON SPOTLIGHT   An imprint of Simon & Schuster Children's Publishing Division   1230 Avenue of the Americas, New York, New York
10020   *Yo Gabba Gabba!* TM & © 2009 GabbaCaDabra LLC. All rights reserved, including the right of reproduction in whole or in part in any
form.   SIMON SPOTLIGHT and colophon are registered trademarks of Simon & Schuster, Inc. For information about special discounts for bulk
purchases, please contact Simon & Schuster Special Sales at 1-866-506-1949 or business@simonandschuster.com.
Manufactured in the United States of America   First Edition 10 9 8 7 6 5 4 3 2 1   ISBN 978-1-4169-7854-1

Hello, friends! It's time to use our imaginations. Close your eyes and picture something in your head—what do you see? Do you know what I see? I see Foofa and Toodee having fun! Let's find out what they are doing.

It's fun to play pretend with friends! And the best thing is
that you can play pretend anytime—by yourself,
when it's raining outside, or even when you're sick.
It's a special power that we all have!

It's time for us to go. But now it's your turn to use your imagination. Remember, you can pretend anything.
What will you do?